George Brown, CLASS CLOWN

Revenge of the Killer Worms

For teachers–unsung heroes who
pay it forward every day–NK

GROSSET & DUNLAP
Penguin Young Readers Group
An Imprint of Penguin Random House LLC

Text copyright © 2015 by Nancy Krulik. Illustrations copyright © 2015 by Aaron Blecha. All rights reserved. Published by Grosset & Dunlap, an imprint of Penguin Random House LLC, 345 Hudson Street, New York, New York 10014. GROSSET & DUNLAP is a trademark of Penguin Random House LLC. Printed in the USA.

Library of Congress Cataloging-in-Publication Data is available.

ISBN 978-0-448-48284-2   10 9 8 7 6 5 4 3 2 1

George Brown, CLASS CLOWN

Revenge of the Killer Worms

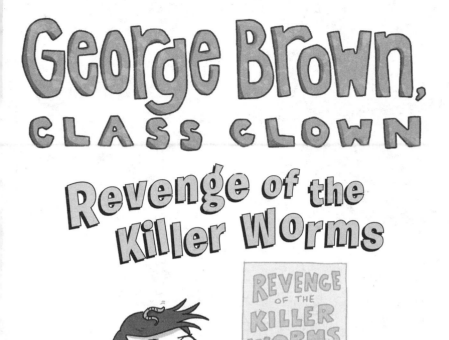

by Nancy Krulik

illustrated by Aaron Blecha

Grosset & Dunlap
An Imprint of Penguin Random House

Chapter 1

"'Supersonic Man versus the Pickled Tomatoes'!" George Brown said as he read the title of the comic book. "This one looks awesome. The **squirty red stuff** looks just like blood."

It was Tuesday afternoon. George and his pals Alex and Chris were hanging out at the Made for Mutants Comic Book Shop.

Chris shook his head.

"I already have that one," he said. "Supersonic Man defeats the tomatoes with **garlic**, the same way you would ward off vampires."

"Sounds like he's making **tomato sauce**," George said. "Maybe he should be called Supersonic *Chef*."

George and Alex started laughing. But not Chris. He took his comic books seriously.

"They must have the one I'm looking for somewhere," Chris said. He started thumbing through another **stack of comics**. "I just have to keep searching."

"Why don't you ask Rodney?" Alex asked Chris. He nodded in the direction of the owner of the store.

"Because looking for just the right comic book is half the fun," Chris explained.

George didn't see what was so fun about searching through stacks and stacks of comic books. Sure, comics were **fun to read**, but this didn't seem all that different from going shopping with his mother. And shopping was boring.

"Hey, what's this?" George asked suddenly. He pointed to a **sheet of paper** taped to the counter. The paper said *Pay It Forward Day Sign-Up Sheet.*

Alex looked over George's shoulder. "It's the sign-up sheet for **Pay It Forward Day**," he said.

"I get that," George replied. "But what's Pay It Forward Day?"

"Oh, right. You moved to Beaver Brook *after* Pay It Forward Day last year," Alex remembered. "It's a **community-service day** we have every year. People help out with things around town. Last year my family helped clean the park. The year before, we painted lampposts."

George looked at the sheet. There were **a lot of things** you could do on Pay It Forward Day—collect coats for needy people, plant flowers around City Hall, read to little kids in the library . . .

"What are you doing *this* year?" he asked Alex.

"We're signed up to serve food to homeless families at the shelter," Alex replied. "You want to come with us?"

"Sure," George agreed. Serving food sounded a lot better than collecting coats or planting flowers. **Food was always fun.**

"You want to help at the shelter this

4

year, too, Chris?" Alex called across the store.

"Okay," Chris answered without looking up from the stacks and stacks of comic books.

"What is it you like so much about this Supersonic dude, anyway?" George asked Chris.

"He's cool," Chris explained. "He has the power to travel through time and space, but he **uses his mind** to fight the bad guys. This one time, he was trapped in a basement with no way out. He found an old metal pipe and turned it into a torpedo. Then he blasted a tunnel and . . ."

Chris kept talking, but George wasn't listening anymore. He was too busy worrying about the **disaster** brewing in his belly. There were bubbles in there. Hundreds of them. And they were going crazy.

That could only mean one thing. The **magical super burp** was back.

George knew that trouble was on its way. After all, it had happened to him many times before. The **burping battles** started right after George's family had moved to Beaver Brook. George's dad was in the army, and his family moved around a lot. Which meant George had been the new kid in school lots of times. So he understood that **first days could be rotten**. But George's first day at Edith B. Sugarman

Elementary had been *super-colossal* rotten!

In his old school, George was the **class clown**. But George had promised himself that things were going to be different this time. No more pranks. No more making funny faces behind teachers' backs. Unfortunately, George didn't have to be a **math whiz** to figure out how many friends a new unfunny kid makes on his first day of school. Zero.

That night, George's parents took him out to Ernie's Ice Cream Emporium just to cheer him up. While they were sitting outside and George was finishing his **root beer float**, a shooting star flashed across the sky. So George made a wish.

I want to make kids laugh—but not get into trouble.

Unfortunately, the star was gone before George could finish the wish. So only half came true—the first half.

A minute later, George had a **funny feeling** in his belly. It was like there were hundreds of tiny bubbles bouncing around in there. The bubbles ping-ponged their way into his chest, and bing-bonged their way up into his throat. And then . . .

George let out a big burp. A *huge* burp. A SUPER burp!

The super burp was loud, and it was *magic*.

Suddenly George **lost control** of his arms and legs. It was like they had minds of their own. His hands grabbed straws and stuck them **up his nose** like a walrus. His feet jumped up on the table and started dancing the hokey pokey. Everyone at Ernie's Emporium started laughing—except George's parents, who were **covered in the ice cream** he'd kicked over while he was dancing.

After that night, the burp came back over and over again. And every time it did, it made a mess of things. That was why George couldn't let that burp **burst out of him** here in the comic book store!

But the bubbles really wanted to come out and play.

Bing-bong. Ping-pong. Already they were beating on his bladder and leaping over his lungs.

George zipped his lips and **pinched his nose**. Bubbles couldn't live without air, could they?

Yes, they could!

Bing-bang. Ping-pang. The bubbles trampled George's tongue. They twisted around his teeth. And then . . .

George opened his mouth and let out a burp. A huge burp. A *supersonic* burp.

Now that the burp was free, George had to do whatever the burp wanted to do. And that was **swing from the rafters**, like Spider-Man swinging from his web.

The next thing George knew, his feet were climbing a tall ladder near a stack of comic books. George's arms reached up and grabbed a wooden rafter. And then he began to swing!

"George, get down from there!" Rodney shouted.

George wanted to get down. But now the burp wanted to swing like **a monkey** in a tree.

"Check me out!" George shouted as he swung from one beam to the next. "I'm Ape Man!" Except George *wasn't* an ape. His arms weren't as strong as a superhero monkey's. Suddenly, George's hands gave way. And then . . .

Slam! George fell from the beam. He landed on the hard floor. Right on his **rear end**. Ouch!

But the burp didn't care that George's butt hurt. All it cared about was playing around in the comic book store. **Burps just want to have fun.** So the next thing George knew, he was climbing up on the counter.

"George Brown, get off the counter!" Rodney shouted.

"Seriously, dude," Alex said, "Get down."

For once, the burp did as it was told. George took a flying leap from the counter. He started **flapping his arms** up and down.

"Look, up in the air!" he shouted. "It's a bird! It's a plane! It's . . ."

Pop! Suddenly, George felt something burst in the bottom of **his belly**. All the air rushed right out of him. The magical super burp was gone.

But George was still there, flying in midair.

Thud.

George landed right on a pile of comic books. They **scattered** all around him.

George opened his mouth to say, "I'm

sorry." And that's exactly what came out.

Rodney looked at the pile of comic books all over the floor and **shook his head**. "You have to leave," he told George.

George didn't blame Rodney for throwing him out. The burp had really made **a mess** of things. He stood up and started for the door.

Suddenly Chris shouted, "There it is! 'Supersonic Man and the Beast from the East'!" He grabbed the comic book from the middle of the scattered pile and handed Rodney money.

"You're the best, George," Chris said as he hurried to get his change and leave with his friends. "I never would have found this on my own."

George shook his head. He didn't feel like the best. **He felt horrible.**

George sure wished there was some superhero who could help him beat the burp once and for all. He could see it now. A **special edition** comic book:

"Supersonic Man and the Battle of the Burps"!

Chapter 2

"It would be a community service if we could figure out a way to **get rid of** my burps," George told Alex as the boys walked into their classroom together Wednesday morning. "I'd stop making a mess of every store in town."

"I'm working on finding a cure," Alex assured him.

Alex was the only other person who knew about George's magical super burps. George hadn't told him what made him act **so weird** sometimes. Alex was just so smart that he'd figured it out on his own.

Lucky for George, Alex was such a good friend that he'd promised to keep the

19

secret and even help George find a cure. So far nothing the boys tried had worked. But if anyone could **find a cure**, a science whiz like Alex could.

As George walked past Mrs. Kelly's desk, he dropped his writing journal on top of the pile. Every kid in the class had a journal. They were supposed to write in it every night. **The journals were private.** The only person who read them was Mrs. Kelly.

George had spent a long time decorating his journal. He'd made a collage with pictures of all his **favorite stars** on the cover. There were photos of snowboard champion Dice Nieveson, skateboard superstar Joe Fovero, and action-movie star Dirk Drek.

"Good morning, everyone," Mrs. Kelly said as the kids took their seats. "I just signed up for this Saturday's Pay It Forward Day. I'm going to be loading backpacks with **school supplies** to send to children whose families can't afford pencils and notebooks. I hope all of you will be participating in this day, too."

"My family is serving dinner at the shelter," Alex said.

"My parents and I are doing that, too," George added.

"My sister and I are cleaning up the park," Julianna said. "My parents are on an **archaeological dig** in Nepal, so they can't be there. But my grandma will be."

"I'm signed up to paint lampposts and mailboxes," Sage said. "But I can come by and **help out** at the shelter afterward. That way *Georgie* and I can serve dinner side by side."

George **rolled his eyes**. *Oh brother.*

"How about you, Max?" Mrs. Kelly asked.

"I don't know," Max said. "I was waiting to see what Louie signed up for."

"That's what *I* was waiting for," Mike said.

Max and Mike really wanted to be like Louie Farley. George couldn't figure out why, though. Louie was kind of **a jerk**.

"I'm not signed up for anything,"
Louie said proudly. "I'm a Farley. We
don't volunteer. We send money."

"Many **charities** need money," Mrs.
Kelly agreed. "But Pay It Forward Day is
about coming together as **a community**.
You might want to think about helping
out somewhere on Saturday."

"Not *this* Saturday," Louie insisted.
"Because I have plans to meet Dirk Drek."

Everyone in the class stared at Louie.

"How are you going to meet him?" George asked. "Dirk Drek lives in Hollywood. That's where he makes his **action movies**."

"He may live in Hollywood now," Louie says. "But he was born in Beaver Brook. Just like me."

"Like me, too," Mike said.

"And me," Max added.

"Like all of us . . . except *George*," Louie said.

George frowned. He hadn't felt like the new kid in a while. Leave it to Louie to make him feel that way again.

"I heard on the radio this morning that Dirk Drek is coming here Saturday for a **special screening** of his new movie, *Revenge of the Killer Worms*," Louie continued. "And I'm going to meet him."

"You have tickets to the screening?"

Mike asked excitedly.

"Of course he does," Max told him. "Who else would have them?"

"Well, I don't actually have tickets . . . yet," Louie admitted. "**But I will.** They're usually only for people in the magazine and newspaper businesses. But I'm sure my dad can get me one."

"Those sorts of **tickets** are tough to come by," Mrs. Kelly warned Louie. "Maybe you should make **other plans** for Saturday. I could use help loading those backpacks."

"My dad can do anything," Louie insisted. "And even if he can't get me a ticket, I'm still going to meet Dirk Drek. There's no way a **movie star** that big can come to town without meeting a Farley."

George tried really hard not to laugh. Louie was ridiculous.

"Well, I wish you luck," Mrs. Kelly told Louie. "Now, if you will all take out your **vocabulary workbooks**, we can get started on this week's word list."

Mrs. Kelly said a lot of other things after that, but George didn't hear any of them. He was **too busy** thinking about Dirk Drek. George was a huge Drek fan. He'd seen all his movies—twice. And he'd put his picture on his journal.

All Louie had on the cover of *his* journal were pictures of **expensive cars**. It wouldn't be fair for Louie to meet Dirk Drek instead of George.

But George was signed up to help out at **the shelter**. And there was no way he could get out of it.

Or *was* there?

Chapter 3

"I'm telling you, Alex," George said later as the boys sat down at a lunch table in the cafeteria. "We could pay it forward by **cleaning out** the movie theater."

"What kind of community service is that?" Alex asked.

"The movie theater is a mess," George said. "You know how much **gum is stuck** under the seats."

"That's what the cleaning crew at the movie theater is for," Alex reminded George.

"But **wouldn't it be cool** if we were cleaning the movie theater at the exact time Dirk Drek got there?" George asked.

"Sure it would be," Alex told him.

George smiled.

"But we're signed up to work at the shelter on Saturday," Alex continued. "They're counting on us."

George frowned. That **wasn't the answer** he was hoping for.

"You're right," George said sadly.

"It just **stinks** that Louie might get to meet Dirk Drek, and I won't."

"Where is Louie, anyway?" Alex wondered.

George looked around. The **whole class** was at the lunch table. But not Louie.

"He said he had to do something," Max said.

"Must have been something very important," Mike told him. "Louie's never late for lunch on **tuna hoagie** day."

George focused on the tuna hoagie on his lunch tray. Canned tuna on bread was a lot more interesting than hearing Max and Mike talk about how great Louie was.

A minute later, Louie appeared at the table with his tray of food.

"Did you do what you needed to, Louie?" Max asked him.

"Yeah," Louie said. "Definitely." He **took a bite** of his sandwich.

Just then, Julianna slid over to where

George and Alex were sitting. "Do you guys want to practice some **soccer moves** at my house after school today?" she asked them.

"Sure," Alex said.

"Why not?" George agreed.

"You mean you're not **skateboarding**?" Louie asked George. "I thought you always worked on your skateboarding moves after school."

George gave Louie a funny look. "What do you care what I do after school?"

"I don't," Louie agreed. "But I understand why you're **giving up** on skateboarding."

"I'm not giving up—" George began.

"I mean, how far can you go on that **dinky old skateboard** you have?" Louie interrupted. "I'm asking my mom to take me over to the sporting-goods store to get me the new Lexithon 210 skateboard. There's not a move I won't be able to do on that board."

"Except you don't know any moves," George said.

"Since when do you skateboard?" Julianna asked Louie.

"Since now," Louie said. "When I saw that board in the window of the sporting-goods store, I knew **I had to have it**." He took the last bite of his hoagie and turned to Max and Mike. "You guys want to go play **killer ball**?" he asked.

Killer ball was a game Louie had made up. He **changed the rules** all the time, so he was always the one who won. No one liked killer ball—except Max and Mike, of course.

"Sure," Max said.

"Count me in," Mike agreed.

As Louie and his pals got up from the table, George shook his head. **"That's strange,"** he said.

"What?" Alex asked him. "You know Max and Mike do anything Louie does."

"No, the whole skateboarding thing," George said. "I just wrote in my journal about the Lexithon 210. I tried it out in the store, and it **was amazing**. But my mom said I had to earn half the money working at Mr. Furstman's pet store on Saturdays before I could have it."

Alex shrugged. "It's probably just a coincidence. Louie couldn't have known anything about what was in your journal. The only person who reads it is Mrs. Kelly. And she would never tell."

"It **makes me crazy** how Louie gets everything he wants," Julianna told George.

George thought about how Louie was going to be free on Saturday to meet Dirk Drek. And how he was going to be the first one in **the whole fourth grade** to own a Lexithon 210 skateboard.

"It makes me crazy, too," George agreed. "Especially since Louie wants the same things *I* do, and I'm not getting *any* of them!"

It really **wasn't fair** that Louie's dad could buy him anything anyone could ever want.

Although, maybe that wasn't completely true. All the money in the world hadn't bought Louie a **decent personality**. He was still pretty much a jerk.

Chapter 4

Ping!

The e-mail alert went off just as George was typing about the **importance of yogurt** for his science nutrition paper. He clicked OPEN in the e-mail icon. It was a **message** from Louie.

HELLO, FANS! Get ready for a brand-new *Life with Louie* webcast. I'm going live in five minutes. It'll be a real good time. So be sure to log on!

Fans? George thought. Did Louie

really think he had *fans*? Other than Max and Mike, nobody liked hanging out with Louie in real life. Why did he think anyone would want to **watch him** on a computer screen?

George looked down at the note cards he had made in the school library. Then he went back to typing his report. *Yogurt is curdled milk that has lots of bacteria. The bacteria coagulates* . . .

George stopped typing. He wasn't sure what the word *coagulate* meant, but it sure **sounded gross**. He started to look it up in the dictionary, but then he glanced at the clock. Just two more minutes until Louie went live on the Web.

There was no reason to **waste any extra time** on Louie Farley. Although . . .

George couldn't help himself. He clicked the link Louie had posted at the bottom of his e-mail. A moment later,

Louie was on his screen.

Well, Louie's *foot,* anyway. Whoever was handling the camera was giving the audience a close-up of one of Louie's **bare feet**. His big toenail looked all yellow. And there was **a wart** or something on his little toe.

"Aim the camera at my face, you idiot," Louie hissed to the cameraman.

"Sorry, Louie," said the cameraman—who sounded like Max—as he raised the camera.

"Hi, everyone," Louie said. "Welcome to *Life with Louie*, the webcast that's all about my life." **He smiled creepily.** "By now you know that Dirk Drek is coming to town this Saturday . . ."

George frowned. He knew, all right.

"A lot of you are going to be volunteering and stuff," Louie continued. "But I won't be. So I'll have **all day** to meet Dirk Drek. I know where he's going to be. I've got his whole schedule." Louie held up a piece of paper.

George shrugged. That was **no big deal**. The schedule was posted on Dirk Drek's website.

"I'm sure I'll get to meet him at one of these stops," Louie said. "When I do, I'll get **his autograph**. Then I'll show it to everybody on another *Life with Louie* webcast."

George was *really* bummed out. Sure, Louie wasn't guaranteed to meet Dirk Drek. But at least he had a chance. George had **no chance at all**. He had to go to the shelter right after his job at the pet shop. And George had to go to the pet shop if he ever wanted to earn enough money for that **new skateboard**.

"I know we're all excited to see Dirk Drek's new movie, *Revenge of the Killer Worms*," Louie continued. "And speaking of **worms**, my dad and I are going fishing in a few weeks. So I've been practicing how to bait a hook."

Louie held up a big bowl. He pointed it toward the camera. Inside the bowl were **a whole bunch** of live worms.

Louie picked up one of the worms and **dangled it** between his fingers. "It's really important that you bait your hook right," he said. "If you don't, the worm will fall off, and you won't catch your fish. You have to shove the **pointed hook** right through the worm at just the right spot—"

BEWWWWW!

George clicked off the computer as fast as he could. He didn't want to see Louie bait the hook with the worm. Just the idea of it **made him feel sick**. It also made him really angry. He raced to the phone and called Alex.

"Hello?" Alex answered.

"Did you see that?" George asked. He didn't even bother to say hi to Alex.

"Oh, hi, George," Alex said. "You mean *Life with Louie*?"

"Yeah," George said. "He's such a jerk."

"You mean because he's **bragging** about not volunteering?" Alex asked.

"Well, that," George agreed. "But also because now I know for sure he's been **reading my journal**. I bet that's why he was late to lunch. He probably sneaked back to the classroom to find out what I wrote in there."

"What makes you think that?" Alex asked.

"I wrote about how I didn't want to go **fishing** with my dad because I couldn't stand the idea of sticking a hook through a worm," George told Alex.

"I wondered why Louie would fill his mom's **fancy soup bowl** with worms," Alex said. "Mrs. Farley's going to be mad when she finds out."

"Not as mad as I am," George said. "Those journals are supposed to be private! I'm telling Mrs. Kelly tomorrow."

"You can't do that," Alex said. "You don't have any proof. I mean, *I* believe you. But Louie could just say it was a **coincidence**. Dirk Drek's new movie *is* called *Revenge of the Killer Worms*. And besides, how would Louie know you were even going to watch his webcast?"

"Yeah, but then that would be *two*

coincidences," George said. "The skateboard and the worms."

"Still—" Alex began.

"There's gotta be a way we can catch him," George interrupted. "Maybe we can **hide a camera** in the classroom and photograph him peeking at my journal."

"Too complicated," Alex said. "But I think there is a way we can prove it."

"How? How?" George asked excitedly. He was really glad he had such a **smart friend**.

"You can write something in your journal that he couldn't possibly have seen or heard anywhere else," Alex began.

"Yeah. And then if he repeats what I wrote . . . or tries to *do* something about what I wrote . . ." George stopped and thought for a minute. Then he shouted, **"I got it!"**

"What?" Alex said.

"I'll tell you tomorrow," George promised. "I gotta go. I have **a trap** to set! I'm going to **catch me** a great big Louie— and I won't even need a worm!"

Chapter 5

"A musical?" Alex repeated as he and George walked to school Thursday morning. "You wrote in your journal that Dirk Drek's next movie is going to be **a musical**?"

George nodded. "I said Dirk was looking for a kid to play his son, and that the kid would have to be able to **dance and sing**. I wrote that I found out about it on a secret website for Dirk Drek's biggest fans."

"You think Louie is going to believe that?" Alex asked. "Dirk Drek is an **action hero**, not a dancer."

"You know how bad Louie wants to be a star," George said. "He's dying to be **famous**. If he thinks he can be in a movie with Dirk Drek, he'll sing and dance like crazy."

"But Louie is a terrible singer. And you saw **how badly** he danced when Mrs. Kelly tried to teach us the Watusi."

"That's the best part," George told him. "If he reads my journal and tries to sing or dance for Dirk, he'll look like a jerk."

Alex looked at George and smiled. **"You're a genius,"** he said. "Mean. But a genius."

George shrugged. "I didn't want to be mean," George told Alex. "But Louie totally **crossed the line**. He has to learn a lesson. He can't just read my private stuff."

"And if he's *not* reading it, he won't do

anything stupid, and he won't look like a jerk," Alex said. "Well, no more than usual, anyway."

"Oh, he's reading it," George assured Alex. "And he's about to **get caught**."

A few minutes later, George walked into his classroom, reached into his backpack, and pulled out his journal. As George dropped the journal off on Mrs. Kelly's desk, he gave Louie **a big smile**.

Louie shot George a dirty look.

"Good morning, everyone,"
Mrs. Kelly said as the kids entered the
room. "Don't get too comfortable. We're
about to line up to go to **the cafeteria**."

"We're having lunch *now*?" Max
asked. "We just had breakfast."

"We're not going to eat," Mrs. Kelly
explained. "The lunch lady is going to
talk to us about nutrition. She's going to
show us what goes into making all the
healthy meals in our cafeteria."

"I don't think I want to know
what goes into cafeteria food," George
whispered to Alex as the kids lined up.
"It's better that **mystery meat** remains a
mystery."

"I'm with you, dude," Alex agreed.

Sage got in line right behind George
and pointed to her T-shirt. "Did you
see my new official Dirk Drek shirt,

Georgie?" she asked. "I thought of you when I bought it. I know **how crazy you are** about Dirk Drek."

George frowned. Sage wasn't the only one in school wearing a **Dirk Drek shirt** today. He had seen at least seven of them on the playground before school started.

Every time George looked at a picture of Dirk Drek's face, he thought about how he wasn't going to **get to meet him**. All this Dirk Drek fever made George feel rotten.

Fever . . . feel rotten . . .

Hey! Maybe that was it. George could **call in sick** to work on Saturday and then try to meet Dirk instead. Or maybe tell Alex he was too sick to work at the shelter.

"Dirk Drek must have a lot of energy," Julianna said, interrupting George's thoughts. "Did you see the **schedule** Louie was talking about on his webcast last night? He'll have to *zoom* around town to make all those stops."

Sage looked around. "Where is Louie, anyway?"

"He had to go to the bathroom," Max said.

"I volunteered to go with him," Mike added. "But he told me he could **do it by himself**."

The kids all laughed. George laughed the hardest. But that was because he was pretty sure Louie wasn't going to the bathroom. More likely, he was going back to the empty classroom to **sneak a peek** at George's journal.

Which was exactly what George wanted him to do.

Chapter 6

"So you think he read it?" Alex asked George as the boys walked past some stores in the center of town after school. "I mean, he **didn't mention** one thing about singing or dancing all day."

"It would be just like Louie to keep the audition information to himself," George told Alex. "He figures if he's **the only one** who knows about it, he'll be the only one to audition. That's less competition."

"I never thought of it that way," Alex admitted.

George smiled. Alex was a whiz at science and math. But when it came to knowing **how rotten** Louie could be,

George was the smart one. That was because George was usually on the receiving end of Louie's rottenness.

"You want to stop at Mr. Tarantella's for **a slice**?" Alex asked.

George frowned. "I don't know," he answered. "Things didn't go so well for me the last time I was in there."

"Oh, I'm sure Mr. Tarantella has forgotten all about that by now," Alex said.

George wasn't so sure. It wouldn't be easy to forget a kid who tossed pizza dough in the air and then let it fall down on his head like a **big gooey mask**.

Still, George was hungry. And he did love pizza.

"I guess we can go," George said. He opened the door and walked into the pizzeria.

"Oh, hello, boys," Mr. Tarantella said

as Alex and George slid into a booth near the window.

George thought Mr. Tarantella sounded **a little nervous**, like he was wondering what George might do this time. George didn't blame him. He wondered that sometimes, too. Because George never knew what **the burp** might make him do. Or when it might make him do it.

"I'll have a slice with pepperoni and a small glass of orange soda," Alex said.

"I'll have the same," George said. "Please." He added the *please* to show Mr. Tarantella that he was trying to be polite.

"Actually, you want **a giant glass** of ice water," Alex told George.

"I do?" George asked.

Alex nodded. "Definitely. Trust me."

As Mr. Tarantella walked back toward the kitchen, George gave Alex a **funny** look. "Why do I want water?" he asked him.

"To drink when you eat this." Alex pulled a **clear plastic bag** out of his backpack. "It's a mix of cumin, dried chili peppers, fennel, and celery. According to the Burp No More Blog I've been following, if you eat this with a big glass of water, your burping will **stop for good**."

George opened the bag and poured the fennel, cumin, chili pepper, and celery into his mouth, chewed, and swallowed.

"Whoa, that's **spicy**," George said. He opened his mouth and stuck out his tongue as he gasped for air.

"It's the chili peppers," Alex said.

"I'm burning up," George croaked.

Just then, Mr. Tarantella brought over Alex's soda and George's water. He took one look at George and rolled his eyes.

George wanted to explain why he had his tongue hanging out. But he couldn't. He was *waaay* too thirsty to talk. So he grabbed the big glass and poured the ice water down his throat in **one gulp**.

"May I have some more water, please?" he asked Mr. Tarantella.

"Uh . . . sure," Mr. Tarantella said. He took George's cup and walked away. A minute later, he returned with another big glass of **cold, icy water**.

"I'm telling you, this is the cure that's gonna work," Alex said.

Now George felt really bad. Here was Alex trying to help him, and George had been thinking about **faking being sick** and bailing on Alex at the shelter. George could never do that to Alex.

He couldn't call in sick to work on Saturday, either. Mr. Furstman was one of the only store owners in Beaver Brook who didn't get upset when the super burp made George do strange things like **eat bugs** or slither around on the floor of the pet shop **like a snake**.

Besides, Mr. Furstman's pet shop was always really busy on Saturdays. Mr. Furstman never had time to feed all the animals. If George didn't show up, the lizards wouldn't have their **crickets** to eat. The hamsters wouldn't have their pellets. And Petey the parrot would have to go seedless.

There was no way George was getting out of either one of those commitments on Saturday. He was just going to have to see Dirk Drek like everyone else—on a movie screen in *Revenge of the Killer Worms.*

"Here you go, boys," Mr. Tarantella said. He placed their pizza slices on the table.

"Thank you," George said. "And thanks for all the water."

"You want some more?" Mr. Tarantella asked him.

George looked down at **his belly**. It was sticking way out because of all the **water sloshing around** in there. "I think I'm okay," he said.

As Mr. Tarantella walked away, Alex looked out the window. "Hey, there's

Louie and his mom," he said.

"He's not coming in here, is he?" George asked.

"No," Alex assured him. "He's going somewhere **down the block**."

"Do you think he's going to Miss Frieda's School of Dance?" George asked excitedly. "To practice for his *audition*?"

"Could be," Alex said. "I can't see from here. It could also be Pansy's Petals Flower Shop, or Hammer and Nails Hardware, or Wally's Workout Sporting Goods. They're all down there."

"Not the **sporting-goods shop**," George groaned. "Because that would mean he's getting the Lexithon 210 skateboard. And he'll bring it to school just to rub it in my face."

"He could still be going to Miss Frieda's," Alex said. "Which would mean he **took the bait**."

George started to smile. But then he stopped. How could he smile when there was something **so awful** going on inside his body?

Slish-slosh. Uh-oh! This was bad. George didn't have much time. He had to get away from the table.

Quickly, George leaped up.

"Oh no," Alex said. **"The burp** again?"

Whoosh-swoosh.

George **crossed his legs** and shook his head. "No," he said. Then he started to run.

"Where are you going?" Alex called after him.

"To the bathroom," George answered. "It's

all that water I drank. I really, really, really, *really* **gotta pee**!"

Chapter 7

"Louie didn't bring a skateboard to school today," Alex whispered to George as they walked into the **school gym** on Friday afternoon.

"I know," George said with a grin. "And check out the way he's walking down the hall. You see how he keeps moving his feet? Toe, heel. Toe, heel. It's almost like he's **tap dancing**."

"Sort of," Alex said. "Of course, his new sneakers could be giving him **blisters**, and that's why he's walking funny."

"It sure looks like dancing," George insisted.

"How's the burp cure going?" Alex asked him.

"So far so good," George said. "I spent a lot of time in the bathroom yesterday. But it will be worth it if I **peed the burp** right out of me."

"Hey! Check it out!" Julianna shouted excitedly as the kids entered the gym. "We're playing volleyball again."

Julianna was the only kid who seemed happy about that. That was because she was the **best volleyball player** in the class.

"I want to be on *her* team this time," George said. "Julianna's team always wins."

"Okay, kids," Coach Trainer said. "Line up and count off by twos."

The kids all got in a straight line. George made sure that when it got to his turn, **he would be a two**—just like Julianna.

Unfortunately, so did Sage. "Oh, Georgie," she squealed as they got in position on the volleyball court. "I just know we're **going to win** with you on our team."

George didn't answer. It was easier to ignore Sage sometimes.

But it wasn't easy to ignore Louie. He kept looking at George from the other side of the net and laughing. For no reason. Just to **psych him out**.

George felt really bad for Alex. Somehow he'd wound up on Louie's team. That couldn't be any fun.

"Okay, you guys, here's the plan," Julianna said. "Aim at Max. He always misses."

George laughed. Julianna was usually a really nice kid. But when it came to sports, she **stopped being nice**. She just wanted to win.

Julianna's strategy worked. Max did miss whenever the volleyball was hit to him. Unfortunately, the other team tried to **hit the ball** to Sage for the same reason. She missed a lot, too. And sometimes even Julianna couldn't leap in to save her. That was how the score wound up at 24–23. George's team **had the lead**.

"Okay, kids," Coach Trainer

said. "This could be for **the game**."

George looked through the net. Louie was serving. So George gave him his best psych-out stare.

Louie stared back and **stuck his tongue out** at George.

No way was George letting Louie's serve keep his team from winning. He bent his knees and got ready, just in case the serve came his way.

And then . . .

Bing-bong. Ping-pong.

Suddenly George felt **something brewing** in the bottom of his belly. Something bouncy. And bubbly. Oh no! The magical super burp was back!

George could not let that burp burst out. Not now. Not in the middle of Louie's serve! Not when it was **game point**!

But the burp didn't care about the volleyball game. It just cared about **bursting out** of George.

Louie held up the volleyball.

The bubbles pranced on George's pancreas.

Louie pulled back his fist.

The bubbles splattered against George's spleen.

George had to do something—quick. He had to force the burp back down toward his feet. Quickly, George flipped upside down into **a handstand.** The bubbles kept traveling up, up, up. Only now *up* was *down!*

"George, what are you doing?" Julianna yelled at him. "Stop fooling around. **Stand up.** This is game point!"

Slam! Louie hit the ball.

From the corner of his eye, George could see the volleyball coming right for him. He knew he should flip back over and **smack the ball** over the net. But he couldn't. Not until the burp was gone.

Louie started to laugh.

George really hated the sound of Louie's laugh. And he hated the idea of Louie's team winning. But he hated the burp even more.

The handstand trick was really working. The bubbles rattled his rib cage. They sneaked around his spleen and knocked into his knees. George's feet **wiggled and wobbled** as he tried to keep his balance. And then . . .

SLAM! George's foot kicked the volleyball. It soared through the air and landed with a thud. **Right at Louie's feet.** Louie had been laughing so hard he'd forgotten to hit the ball.

Pop! Suddenly, George felt something burst in his belly. All the air rushed out of him. The magical super burp was gone. *All right!* George had **squelched the belch**! And scored the game point!

"YES! WE WON!" Julianna shouted excitedly.

"NO, YOU DIDN'T!" Louie shouted back. Then he stopped and looked at Coach Trainer. "George cheated," he whispered.

"I did not," George insisted. Which was true. If anyone had **cheated**, it was the magical super burp. But George wasn't even sure the burp had done anything wrong.

"Yes, you did," Louie whispered to him.

"Why are you whispering?" Max asked Louie.

"I'm saving my voice," Louie said quietly.

"For what?" George asked him.

"None of your **beeswax**," Louie hissed. He turned to Coach Trainer. "You saw George kick the ball, right?"

Coach Trainer nodded. He leafed through the pages of his **phys-ed coach handbook**. "But there's nothing in here that says he can't do that. As long

as it's a clean hit, the ball can bounce off any part of your body."

"That means WE WIN!" Julianna shouted again.

"Thanks to Georgie," Sage added. She **batted her eyelashes** at George.

George wasn't paying any attention to Sage. He was too busy listening to Louie whisper his complaints to Coach Trainer.

Louie might not be telling anyone why he was whispering, but George was pretty sure he knew why. Louie was trying to **save his voice** for his big movie-musical audition. An audition that would never happen!

George grinned. This was turning out better than he'd ever imagined. Because on top of everything else, he wouldn't have to hear Louie's **annoying voice** for the rest of the day!

Chapter 8

"George, can you go in the stockroom and grab a **bag of birdseed**?" Mr. Furstman asked George early Saturday morning. It was already the fourth time that day that Mr. Furstman had sent George back to the stockroom for something. The store was **really busy**. It was a good thing George had come to work instead of pretending to be sick so he could catch a glimpse of Dirk Drek. Mr. Furstman really needed him.

As George walked into the storeroom, he glanced at the small TV Mr. Furstman had mounted on the wall. The **news reporter** on the screen was talking about how many people were volunteering that day.

"These kids are busy painting our lampposts a **vivid green**," the reporter said. Suddenly, Sage's face popped on the screen. She smiled and waved her paintbrush. Green paint **splattered** all over the news reporter's suit.

The reporter jumped back. "What are you doing?" he shouted, forgetting he was on TV. Sage **stopped smiling**. But George didn't. He thought it was hilarious.

The TV droned on as George walked over to the shelves and grabbed a heavy bag of birdseed. He started to head back toward the front of the store when suddenly he heard a different TV reporter say, "I'm here outside the WBVB radio station, where **hometown hero** Dirk Drek has just completed an interview. Dirk is in town to promote his new movie, *Revenge of the Killer Worms*."

George stopped for a minute and looked at **the crowd** outside the radio station. There seemed to be at least a hundred people outside watching as Dirk got into his limo to go to his next stop. Cameras were flashing. People were cheering and shouting.

Suddenly, in the middle of the crowd,
George spotted a **familiar face**. It was
Louie. He was jumping up and down and
waving his hands wildly, trying to get
Dirk's attention. He looked like a jerk.
And he wasn't getting anywhere
near Dirk Drek.

But, then again, neither
was George.

"Dirk! Dirk! Dirk!"

Later that day, as
George walked to the
shelter, he heard people
screaming in the streets.

"Dirk! Dirk! Dirk!"

"Is Dirk Drek here?"
George asked a man who was
standing at the edge of the
huge crowd that had gathered.

"He's having **lunch** in the

Pita Pan Sandwich Shop down the block,"
the man said.

"Why would a big movie star go to a **sandwich shop** for lunch?" George asked.

"He said it was his favorite place to go after school when he was growing up," the man explained.

"Have you seen him yet?" George asked the man.

"Nah," the man replied. "The crowd's too big. And all the **news crews** are

blocking the windows because they can't
get inside. Dirk Drek's rented out the
whole restaurant so that he can eat lunch
without **cameras in his face**."

George thought about waiting around
to see if he could catch a **glimpse** of Dirk
when he finished eating. But it was getting
late. And he had to get to the shelter.

Quickly, he tried to push his way

through the crowd. It wasn't easy. The people there were **squished tight** together. And no one wanted to move. Not even a little.

"Mommy mee ma moo. Mommy mee ma moo."

As George scrunched his way between a crowd of teenagers and a big guy who smelled like a mix of **onion breath and feet**, he heard a terrible screeching sound.

"Mommy mee ma moo!"

Wait a minute. George was sure he had heard that voice before.

"Louie! Is that you?" George shouted through the crowd.

Suddenly the **squawking** stopped.

"What are you doing here?" Louie asked. At least, George thought it was Louie. He couldn't see him through the crowd. "Go away. We don't want Dirk

Drek to meet the town **weirdo freak**!"

Yeah. That was definitely Louie.

Louie began squawking again.
"Naaaayyyy . . . ," he cackled.
"Naaaayyyy . . ."

Now he sounded like a **wicked witch**. That was strange. George hadn't written anything in his journal about a witch being in Dirk Drek's next movie.

Was it possible Louie *hadn't* read George's journal?

George wasn't sure how to feel about that. On the one hand, it would be nice if George's secrets were still secrets. But on the other hand, it would be fun to have Louie make a **real fool** out of himself in front of Dirk Drek, the news cameras, and half of Beaver Brook.

"Nay naaaaay naaaayyy . . ." Louie began cackling again. *"Mommy mee ma moo."*

Okay, now who was acting like the town freak? George shook his head. Something **very strange** was going on with Louie.

Then again, there was always something kind of strange about Louie.

Chapter 9

"Where have you been, dude?" Alex asked as George walked into the shelter. "We're just about to start **serving dinner**."

"I didn't think you were gonna make it," Chris added.

"I'm sorry," George apologized. "There were **a lot of people** on the streets. Are my parents here yet?"

"They're in the kitchen," Chris said. "The grown-ups are cooking, and the kids are serving."

Alex handed George a pair of **plastic gloves and a hairnet**. "We gotta wear these," he said.

George looked at the net. "You're kidding," he said.

Alex shook his head. "Nope. It's a rule." He slipped his net over his hair.

"I feel like the **lunch lady**." George frowned as he put his net on, too. This day was going from bad to worse.

"Hi, Georgie!"

Suddenly, the day went from bad to worse to *absolute worst*. Sage was here.

"I'm so glad I finished painting in time to help serve dinner," she said. "It's **going to be fun** working together. Don't you think so?"

George did *not* think so. Not one bit.

Just then a woman in a white dress entered the room. "Can I have your attention?" she said. "My name is Jane Samson. I'm the director of the Beaver Brook family shelter. I want to thank you for **volunteering** to help us serve dinner to our families. I know this is going to be the best Pay It Forward Day ever!"

The kids all cheered. Then they put on their gloves, stepped behind serving trays, and waited for the families to enter the dining room. Alex stood by the tray holding the **peas and carrots**. George stood by the corn on the cob. Sage squeezed her way next to George and got ready to serve slices of turkey. Chris headed to the end of the line to serve cookies.

"Here come the people," Alex said happily.

George couldn't understand what Alex was so excited about. They were standing behind trays of **steaming-hot food** and wearing hairnets. What was so great about that?

Just then, the doors to the dining room opened. A **crowd** of people rushed in.

George knew that the people who lived at the shelter didn't have homes, but he wouldn't have been able to tell that just by looking at them. These people looked like **regular families**. Moms, dads, and kids. Just like George and his family.

"Can I have an extra ear of corn?" one little boy asked George hopefully. "It's my favorite."

"Sure," George said. He used the metal tongs to plop another **ear of corn** on the boy's plate.

The boy smiled so wide, George could see every single one of **his teeth**. "Gee, thanks!" he said.

The boy's smile made George smile.

Another little boy in a blue shirt came up to where Alex was standing. "Hey, kid, you want to be as **big and strong** as Dirk Drek?" Alex asked him.

"Yes!" the boy answered.

"Then you have to eat peas and carrots," Alex said. "That's Dirk Drek's **secret**. They make him strong."

"Give me lots!" the little boy told Alex.

Alex plopped a heaping spoonful of vegetables on the boy's plate.

"Thanks, mister," the little boy said.

George laughed. It was **funny** hearing a kid call Alex *mister*. Alex was just a kid, too.

An older woman with **gray hair** slid her tray in front of George. She looked really tired, and she had a small hole in her **sleeve**.

George put a piece of corn on a plate and placed it on the woman's tray. "Would

PEAS + CARROT

you like two?" he asked her.

The woman shook her head. "No, thanks. One's plenty." She looked down at her tray and smiled. "Turkey, vegetables, *and* corn. This is the **best meal** I've had in a long time."

Wow. George shook his head. His mom made turkey, vegetables, and corn pretty often. He hadn't thought of it as **anything special**—until now.

As the woman moved on, a little girl with **long brown braids** slid her tray over to George and looked down at the ground.

"Hey, I bet you like corn on the cob," George said to her. "Do you want two?"

The **little girl** didn't answer. She just kept staring at the floor.

"Melissa's **kind of quiet**," the man beside her said. "She hasn't said a word since we arrived here yesterday. I think she's **scared**. This is the third shelter our family has stayed in this year."

Wow. If anyone understood how tough moving could be, it was George. But even his family hadn't moved three times in one year. And at least every time they'd moved, it had always been to **a house**. Not a shelter. No wonder Melissa seemed so sad.

"Do you think an extra ear of corn would **make her happy**?" George asked Melissa's dad.

"It's worth a shot," her dad said.

"Do you want more corn?" George asked her.

Melissa **shook her head** sadly.

George frowned as Melissa and her father walked away. He felt really bad for her.

A teenage girl slid her tray over to

George. "Corn, please," she said.

"Sure," George replied. He **plopped**
an ear of corn on her plate.

"Can I get two?" the teenage girl asked
George. "We **hardly ever** get fresh corn for
dinner."

"Sure," George said. He plopped
another ear of corn on her tray. And then
another.

"Three?" the teenage girl said, surprised. "Thanks."

Just then, Jane Samson walked over to Alex and George. "Your trays are **almost empty**," she said. "Better go back into the kitchen and get some more."

"Yes, ma'am," Alex said.

"Okay," George added. He followed Alex into the kitchen.

"Isn't Pay It Forward Day fun, dude?" Alex said.

George nodded. "I'm glad I—"

George stopped talking mid-sentence. He **zipped his lips** tight. He couldn't let another word slip out. Because if he did, the burp that had just started bouncing around in his belly might slip out, too.

And that would be *baaaad!*

Chapter 10

Bing-bang. Cling-clang.

The **bubbles were back** in George's belly. They were bouncing up and down and all around. Already they were kicking at George's kidneys and alley-ooping over his arteries.

Ding-doing! Zing-zoing!

The bubbles slipped between George's shoulders and climbed up his clavicle. They **trampled onto his tongue** and licked at his lips. And then . . .

BUUURP!

George let out a huge burp. A super burp. A burp so loud, and so powerful, it **rattled** all the pans in the kitchen.

"Dude, no!" Alex shouted.

Dude, yes. The burp was free. Now George had to do whatever the burp wanted to do.

"George!" his mother scolded. "What do you say?"

George opened his mouth to say, "Excuse me." But that's not what came out. Instead George shouted, "It's **turkey trot** time!"

The next thing he knew, George was shoving his hand into a whole turkey. Then his feet started trotting out into the dining room.

"George! Put down that turkey!" his dad shouted. "That's an order."

Uh-oh. A direct order! George knew he had to listen to his dad now.

But burps don't **take orders** from anyone. So George kept running, right over to the table where Melissa was sitting with her dad. He started bouncing the turkey up and down like a **hand puppet** putting on a show.

"Gobble! Gobble!" George said.

"Dude, that's gross," Alex said. "You've got your hand in that **turkey's tush**."

That *was* gross. But gross is what burps like best.

"Gobble! Gobble!" George said again.

Melissa began to smile. And then she began to laugh.

Everyone in the dining room stopped to look at her.

"Do it again," Melissa said in a quiet little voice.

George picked up an ear of corn from Melissa's dad's tray and **shoved it in his ear**.

"What did you say?" he asked her. "I couldn't hear you. There's an ear in my ear."

Melissa giggled.

The turkey on George's hand **wiggled**. The corn in his ear jiggled.

And then . . . *Pop!* George felt something pop in the bottom of his belly. All the air rushed out of him. The magical super burp was gone. But George was still there. With a **turkey on his hand** and corn in his ear.

Jane Samson raced over. "Young man!" she scolded. "Food is not a toy!"

George pulled the ear of corn from his ear. He opened his mouth to say, "I'm sorry." And that's exactly what came out.

"Thank you for **making my daughter smile**," Melissa's dad said to George.

Jane Samson sighed. "Food isn't meant to be played with," she told George. George frowned. He felt **really bad**. "But you made this little girl happy for the first time in a long time," Jane Samson continued. "And that's definitely worth something."

George smiled. That made him feel a little better.

"Now, please get back in the serving line," Jane Samson told George. "And don't cause **any more trouble**. If you do, I will have to ask you to leave."

"I won't," George promised. He walked back toward the food trays.

"Dude, I really gotta find you a **cure** that works," Alex whispered as George got back in line beside him.

"No kidding," George replied.

"But at least it wasn't all bad this time," Alex said. "You—"

Alex never got to finish his sentence, because at just that moment, the dining-room doors **swung open**. A group of people rushed inside. Some had cameras. Others held microphones. And **right in the middle** of the crowd . . .

"Is that who I think it is?" George asked Alex excitedly.

"Yep," Alex said. "Dirk Drek is in the house!"

"What's he doing *here*?" George wondered out loud.

"Maybe **he's hungry**," Sage suggested.

Jane Samson walked over to Dirk. "Mr. Drek, can I help you?" she asked.

"I'm here to help *you*," Dirk answered. "After all, it's Pay It Forward Day. And **when I was a kid**, this is where my family helped out."

Dirk walked over to where George and his friends were standing. The camera crews and news reporters followed close behind.

"You mind if I **help you** serve this corn on the cob?" Dirk asked George.

George didn't answer. He couldn't. His mouth wasn't working. So he just nodded his head.

"Great," Dirk said. He squeezed in beside George.

"Excuse me, Mr. Drek?" Alex held up **a hairnet**. "You're supposed to wear one of these."

Everyone in the room laughed. Dirk Drek **laughed the hardest**.

"Okay," he said as he slipped the net over his hair. "But please, call me Dirk. What are your names?"

CORN

he asked George and Alex.

George just stared at him. He was **so excited**, he couldn't remember.

"His name is George," Alex said. "And I'm Alex."

"Okay, George and Alex," Dirk Drek said, slipping on a pair of gloves. **"Let's get moving.** We've got hungry people here."

George nodded and placed an ear of corn on the next tray as it came through. Then he looked up again to see if Dirk Drek was still there. Yup. There he was. This wasn't **a dream**—even though it felt like one.

It was too bad Louie wasn't there. It would have really made him crazy to see George standing right next to Dirk Drek in the food line.

Still, this was the **best day ever**! Nothing could top this.

George picked up a hot ear of corn with the metal tongs. He started to place it on the next tray. And then . . .

BAM! The dining-room doors flew open—again!

"It don't mean a thing if it ain't got that swing!"

Louie ran into the dining room. Well, not ran, exactly. It looked like he was dancing. He was **tapping his feet** up and down, waving a big top hat in the air, and singing.

"Doo-ah, doo-ah, doo-ah!"

George looked at Alex. Alex looked at George. Both boys began to laugh.

"He fell for it!" George exclaimed.

Louie tapped his feet up and down. He **tossed his hat** in the air, reached up his arms, and . . . missed it completely.

"Young man! What are you doing?" Jane Samson asked.

Louie stopped mid-dance. "I'm
auditioning for Dirk Drek's **new movie
musical**," he told her. "Wait, I can do
it better. Let me warm up my voice.

Mommy mee ma moo. Nay nay nay."

So that was what Louie had been doing outside the sandwich shop. Vocal warm-ups.

Louie started **singing and dancing** again. *"It don't mean a thing—"*

"What movie musical?" Dirk interrupted him.

"Your **big secret project**," Louie said as he tap-danced. "The *real* reason you're in town."

"I don't know what you're talking about," Dirk told him. "Where did you hear I was filming a musical?"

Louie looked over at George and Alex. His face turned **beet red**.

"Yeah, Louie," George said. "Where did you hear that?" He and Alex laughed even harder.

Louie picked up his top hat and stormed toward the door.

Click-clack. Click-clack. Louie's tap

shoes made **loud noises** as he stomped away.

Click-clack. Click-clack.

"WHOAAAA!" Suddenly, Louie slipped on **turkey grease**. He slid across the floor.

Crash! Louie slid into one of the tables in the dining room.

Bam! He **landed face-first** in Melissa's dad's tray.

Melissa giggled.

George and Alex laughed harder. George laughed so hard, **he snorted**.

Soon everyone in the room was laughing. Well, everyone except Louie, anyway. He was just standing there, wiping **turkey gravy** out of his eyes.

"Who would believe *I* would make a movie musical?" Dirk Drek said.

George smiled. "Louie would."

"I wonder where he heard that," Dirk said.

George didn't answer. He'd never tell.

George looked up at Dirk Drek. His movie-star hero was right there, serving corn on the cob—just like a normal person.

Then George looked over at Louie. He was **picking a pea out of his nostril** and trying to hide his face from the news cameras.

George grinned. It turned out that the best day ever *could* get better, after all.

George was glad he hadn't figured out a way to get out of working at the shelter. He was actually having a really good time. **It felt great** to hear people say how happy they were to have a good meal. And it was awesome that he was able to make Melissa laugh. Nothing could spoil this day now.

Gurgle-groan. Schmurgle-moan.

George gulped. Uh-oh. **Not the burp!** Not again. Not with Dirk Drek standing right next to him!

Gurgle. Schmurgle.

Wait a minute. George didn't feel any bubbles bouncing around. This wasn't a burp, after all. It was just **hunger pangs**. *Phew.*

Boy, George really hated that burp. And the worst part was, he was afraid that no matter what he did, no one would ever be able to stop it.

Not someone as smart as Alex.

Not even someone as powerful as Dirk Drek. Because a superstar action-movie hero might be able to defeat **killer worms** . . . but he was no match for a magical super burp!

About the Author

Nancy Krulik is the author of more than 150 books for children and young adults, including three *New York Times* Best Sellers and the popular Katie Kazoo, Switcheroo books. She lives in New York City with her family, and many of George Brown's escapades are based on things her own kids have done. (No one delivers a good burp quite like Nancy's son, Ian!) Nancy's favorite thing to do is laugh, which comes in pretty handy when you're trying to write funny books! You can follow Nancy on Twitter: @NancyKrulik.

About the Illustrator

Aaron Blecha was raised by a school of giant squid in Wisconsin and now lives with his family by the south English seaside. He works as an artist designing funny characters and illustrating humorous books, including the one you're holding. You can enjoy more of his weird creations at www.monstersquid.com.